BETE NOIRE
FEAR IS JUST A POINT OF VIEW

Editors:

A. W. Gifford
Jennifer L. Gifford

P.O. Box 1013
Gayson, Ga 30017

www.betenoiremagazine.com

Bete Noire is published by Dark Opus Press a division of Charm Noir Omnimedia P.O Box 1013, Grayson, Ga 30017

ISBN: 978-0615603674

In This Issue

URsUs HORRIBILis

Christian Riley

The raw soil crunches under the weight of me, but I am still hungry none the less. Very hungry. That salmon-run seemed just a little bit too...sparse this year.

Probably because of *them*.

Yet things aren't right. Not good. The snow will soon arrive, and I need to be fat. Real fat to fight off all that cold I'll be facing way up there on the mountain.

More berries and grass this morning. The taste is divine, often the best around, but certainly not enough. Not nearly enough.

Sometimes those wolves leave a few scraps for me. Busted up elk or caribou. Even a moose, on a good year. But not this time. Not this year anyways. Or the last...Or even the one before that.

Truth be told, I haven't so much as caught wind of my forest friends for a long time now. Not sure where they all went.

Captured a chipmunk today. Had a real nice texture and crunch, but the taste was off. Sort of bland, lacking spice and flavor. Must have been a young one. Maybe I'll head back down to the river, see if there aren't any stragglers swimming up-stream. I'll be sure to keep my eye out for any young cubs also. But then again, maybe not. If their mama is as hungry as I am, she'll be itching for a fight.

...Oh, for the love of Mother Nature...More of *them*.

Why the hell are they here anyways? They don't even take the fish half the time. Just pull them out of the water, cheer a little bit as they slap each other's paws, then let the salmon go back.

I don't get it.

They sure get all uppity when we come around though. When we get close to them at least. Last year I watched as old Bob ran off into the woods howling with anger. One of them sprayed him with a weird device, leaving Bob's eyes stinging for days. It was funny sure enough, seeing Bob run like that, but he died later because of it. Died of hunger on account that he was too scared to go back and fill-up on fish.

But if we don't get too close...if we keep our distance as I'm sure they would like us to do, they almost seem to blend-in around here.

Well, not quite. Only the ones who quietly stand there in the water, like little dumb trees rooting in the middle of a river. They blow it when they walk though. Or when they make their noises to each other. Or when they drift along in those shiny boxes, throwing that stick out and away from them, using it to pull up a fish...

My fish.

Actually, they're as clumsy and foolish as a lamed-up buck during the Rut. They only pretend to blend-in really. Standing there in the river, or on a trail with a calmness that seems almost convincing. Convincing to them maybe, but not to us. We know them for what they aren't. For what they want to be perhaps, but will never achieve with all that crap they haul around. All that "unnatural" stuff which they apparently can't live without.

They don't belong here.

Look...there goes one now, traipsing along over there on the opposite shore.

Ha! It sees me.

Now it's pointing one of those little shiny things at me again...Yep, and there goes that sound...something like the snapping of a twig.

They don't smell right either. There's a common muskiness about them, but they all seem to have their own "flowery" fragrance lingering around as well. Whatever that's about?

I wonder what they would smell like while they ran in fear for their lives...terrified? Scared to death.

Better yet...

That one over there actually looks kind of yummy, now that I think about it. Got some rolls of blubber jouncing along as it walks...like a little harbor seal on two legs.

Hmmm...Maybe I'll go back here into the woods and watch from a distance.

I know they can be dangerous though. They've got those sticks which kill when they point them at us. Not sure how that works, but I've seen it happen. They come up here all the time using those sticks on the deer, and the moose.

But that one doesn't seem to have one of those sticks.

It thinks I left now. I can tell 'cause it's got that "calmness" look on its face again. Yeah, and now it's trying to catch a fish.

Hmmm...it appears to be by itself also. Maybe I'll just wait here and watch for awhile.

Interesting. Aside from those "kill sticks" of theirs, they hardly look threatening at all. They don't appear to have any sharp claws or jagged teeth like a cougar. They certainly can't run off like an antelope...not with all that stuff they carry on them. Actually, they look pretty slow and awkward with just simply walking around. Like an old caribou sick with age, unable to keep up with the rest of the herd. Unable to even run.

Hmmm...Just waiting to die and get eaten.

But maybe they fight like a badger.

Hey look, there it goes now. It'll be dark soon, and they don't ever hang around here when it gets dark. Most of them get back in those shiny boxes and tear off down river. But not this one. It's walking down that trail...by itself.

I'll keep my distance so it won't know I'm following.

Wow. This is easier than I thought it would be. Between its ridiculous smell and clumsy walk along this trail, I could probably follow this creature from miles away...Oh, but it stopped now.

I've seen these places before. Little clearings where they sleep for the night. Sometimes they set up those colorful, mushroom-looking caves in which they crawl into as well. And when it gets dark, they always make their fire. Guess I'll just sit down again...watch for a while.

Not sure what it's eating now, but it definitely smells good. Some type of meat, with lots of spice, and lots of flavor no doubt...

Oh, now it's shoving something that smells like honey into its mouth. My goodness, this is almost too much. Hope he can't hear my stomach growling over here in these bushes.

Look at that. Now it's getting itself ready for sleep. No den though...just a big bag under the sky, right next to that fire. And yes, it's still all by its lonesome self.

I can hardly wait.

It's funny how they growl when they're sleeping. Not a loud growl though. Not like *my growl*. Just enough to say 'Hey, I'm asleep now...so why don't you come on over here and eat me.'

Hmf..! Not so bad after all. Found out that "it" was a "he", and he certainly didn't fight like no badger. Just made a mess of noise...up until I bit into his neck and shook him a bit. Shoot! He was almost as easy to kill as that chipmunk was earlier, and much tastier by far. Guess I'll have to tell the others about this. One thing is for certain though...a few more of them, and I'll be right as rain for the upcoming snow way up there on the mountain.

Hmmm...how 'bout that. Now there's a warm thought to go along with this toasty fire he left me.

Beginning at 5:00 a.m., Chris spends the only available lot of solitary time he gets in a day feeding his addiction to writing. If he's lucky, he'll get two hours in before "they" wake up, after which he lives a wonderful life as a family man. Since picking up this new habit a few months ago, he has had one story published at The Horror Zine, and five more forthcoming at various publishers. He can be reached at chakalives@gmail.com.

TRUE BELIEVER

Ed Cooke

Outside in the sunshine my neighbours caught a Believer. I wondered where they had found her—or him; I had heard both sexes scream often enough since the Fall.

Nancy from Number 14 chaired our Residents' Association. I heard her jarring tones very clearly through my garage door. She had used that same grinder of a voice on me when I refused to join. Mob violence isn't my scene: nobody gets Redeemed that way.

"You are a Believer!" Nancy grated. The purple skin and red eyes on the poor schmuck must have been evidence enough, but Nancy liked to do things by the book. For all I knew she had a secretary taking minutes. "God has smiled on you and turned His face from us. He has proved Himself unjust. But we will have justice!"

I listened to the Association's justice raining down on the Believer right in front of my up-and-over door, a crude squall of bats and fists and feet. Each blow reminded me why I do not hunt with the pack.

I tightened the last of the vices on my workbench. Then I said softly, so the neighbours would not hear, "Do you recant your faith in God, Father, Son and Holy Spirit, and renounce your claim on His heavenly kingdom?"

By the light of the fluorescent tube the woman's flesh, ordinarily purple-hued as a sign of her belonging to the coming kingdom, took on the bruised colour of aubergine. She was keeping her eyes closed but I knew she was awake: the last of the icy water was still dripping on to the concrete floor. She had every right to resist; no true Believer would turn lightly from the narrow path.

My car was long since burnt out, but no one in his right mind tried to drive anywhere these days. I was only glad I had kept hold of a spare battery for it. I closed the circuit briefly before I put the question again.

She started babbling then, and I was disappointed when I made out the usual wild claims about a virus. I shook my head and tutted softly. "I have no idea how you got picked out for Heaven, telling lies like that. I could have come up with something much more convincing. Perhaps that's how come I'm not among the elect. Yet."

I left her to think about that while I went to consider the array of tools hung on the walls and ceiling. Frankly, I was running out of ideas. What I needed now was divine inspiration. I smiled grimly at the thought, closed my eyes and picked an instrument at haphazard.

At sight of it, she became much more communicative. "Where's Michael? My husband? Are you going to do this to him too?"

"Martyred already. There was nothing I could do to persuade him to apostatise. Believe me, I tried my hardest. I'm hoping you will see reason."

"We weren't even Christians. Before we — before we got sick. But we did what we thought was right, what anyone would have done."

"Tell the truth! Why did I have to force you out of your chapel at gunpoint? Why do you Believers always lock yourselves in holy places, if not to keep out the dirty and defiled?"

"The religious folks welcomed us in. After the hospitals closed their doors. Churches were our isolation wards, so this contagion would end with us. Why didn't you leave us to die?"

Lies kept on pouring out, lies to test me. I smiled and inserted my earplugs.

My work had hardly begun when I felt my heart strangely warmed, just as my forebears in faith had described. I was overjoyed to see bruises swell up on my palms. They began to weep, and so did I.

Stigmata. Thank you, Jesus. Thank you for saving me.

Ed Cooke *plays bass with prog rock band* Voyager Project. *His short film script* Embargo *was produced as a fundraiser for Diabetes UK. He is currently working on his second novel.*

THE SHADOW THIEF

Bruce Boston

The shadow thief
yanks you into an alley,
presses a knife
against your throat,
and demands you empty
your pockets completely.

He picks and chooses
at his pleasure.

The shadow thief takes
the watch from your wrist
and places it on his own,
pausing to admire
it for a moment
in ritual satisfaction.

The shadow thief
materializes a syringe
from his shabby overcoat
or shiny leather jacket.
By a swift jab of the spike
he anesthetizes you
instantaneously.

With that selfsame knife,
sharp and unclean,
in that selfsame alley,
dark and unclean,
the shadow thief
skillfully extricates
one of your organs
for sale on the black market.

The shadow thief
yanks you into an alley,
presses a knife
against your throat,
and demands you empty
your pockets completely.
He picks and chooses
at his pleasure.

He excavates the sum
of your hidden fears.

The shadow thief
has no need for your soul,
with that he will leave you,
naked and shivering,
bloody and violated,
in the long night
shadows of the city.

Bruce Boston *is the author of forty-five books and chapbooks, including the novels* The Guardener's Tale *and* Stained Glass Rain. *His writing has received the Bram Stoker Award, a Pushcart Prize, the Asimov's Readers Award, and the Grand Master Award of the Science Fiction Poetry Association*

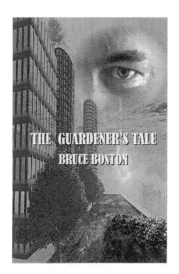

The Light Sponge Maneuver

Caroline Cormack

"Avon House Hotel, how can I help you?

"Yes, this is the manager speaking. Who is calling?

"Of course Mr. Culpin, let me just check for you.

"Here it is sir. Don Richards. Checked in on Wednesday.

"No problem at all, sir. I'll get right on that.

"Goodbye."

"Goedenmorgen. Rembrandt Hotel, hoe kan ik u helpen?

"Yes, I speak English. May I help you?

"One minute."

"This is the manager, how may I help?

"Yes, Mr. Culpin, I've heard of you. How may we be of assistance?

"Let me check with reception.

"Yes, we have a Dennis Roberts staying here.

"I see.

"Yes I understand. I'll do that now.

"Our pleasure Mr. Culpin. Good morning."

"Hello, Sea View?"

"Mr. Culpin sir, is there a problem?

"Yes, he checked in this morning.

"*Okay. I'll call Bob if he checks out.*
"*Will do. Good bye.*"

Mrs. Crosby and Mrs. Fitch met on the train station as they had planned. The other people waiting on the platform paid them no heed. They appeared to be nothing more than two old ladies off for a day out at the beach; two of many such women, with their sturdy shoes and pastel-colored raincoats, filling the days of retirement as best they could.

The two women were in their late sixties. Mrs. Crosby was the taller and thinner of the pair, she wore her grey hair pinned back in a no-nonsense bun and carried a small black suitcase. Mrs. Fitch, the shorter, rounder and friendlier of the two women, was not as business-like in her choice of accessories: she carried a large carpet bag, which led to a good ten minutes of rummaging every time she needed to find anything.

"Hard to tell it's June from the weather." Mrs. Fitch moaned as they waited for the train. She looked up at the drizzle, which was threatening to get worse.

"Good lord, is it June already?" Mrs. Crosby said looking at the date on her watch. It was a chunky man's watch and Mrs. Crosby didn't like it very much, but the dial was large and the numbers were big and clear so she could read them easily. "This plan was so last minute I just had it in my head as being on Thursday and didn't really register the date. The year is just flying by."

At last their train pulled in to the station. A young man helped the two ladies with their luggage. He assured them he was riding all the way to Southbourne himself and would be there to help them get their bags back down from the overhead racks. If he had been surprised at the weight of the suitcase he hadn't said anything. Mrs. Crosby thought she spotted a flicker of surprise as he picked it up. One could always rely on male vanity to keep quiet.

Once the two ladies had arrived in Southbourne, they set out to look for a nice teashop so they could sit down and review their plans for the day.

Sitting at a table by the window of the teashop, Mrs. Crosby pulled a pretty folder with a delicate blue flower pattern from her suitcase. At home she used plain manila ones, but kept a pack of flowered folders and other stationery for use in public. Two old ladies planning a cake sale; that's all people would see if they glanced over. Nothing worth a second look.

The two women re-read their file on the man they had first heard about five days previously. His name was David Robinson, he was forty-three, had a wife, two kids and a mountain of debt with the sort of people who don't allow payment holidays. It was the usual story: he'd wanted to borrow some money to expand his arcade and bingo business and a checkered credit--not to mention criminal--history meant that the normal routes of borrowing were closed to him. He had accepted an investment from George Culpin, the man behind most of the shady enterprise in the area.

Based out of Brighton, Culpin had started in business after the Second World War, just running a few hotels at first and, through hard work and plenty of violence, he'd built himself a tidy little empire all along the south coast.

When profits from the new schemes didn't materialize, Robinson tried gambling his way out of debt. That was no more successful than his business enterprise and pretty soon he was in a hole he couldn't get out of.

None of which called for the involvement of these two most particular old ladies, but then Robinson tried to get himself out of debt by skimming off the take for George Culpin and that was a problem that needed solving.

For his investment, Culpin had taken the title of the properties where Robinson operated his businesses and took a percentage of the take as a weekly operating fee on top of a rental charge. Even George Culpin couldn't keep an eye on every transaction that went on in the daily running of his business, and Robinson had managed to get away with under-paying on the percentage for almost a year before suspicions were raised. Culpin sent his auditors in to thoroughly review the business' books.

The local area boss who hadn't spotted the scam when it first started had made amends by reporting the loss as soon as he found it and paying full restitution to Mr. Culpin. As such, Culpin was inclined to be magnanimous. Everyone can make a mistake. Once. The local man got the message and Culpin was sure he'd never see similar difficulties on that man's patch again.

For David Robinson, however, no such generosity was available. Robinson had sought to solve his problems by stealing from Mr. Culpin. Worse, he hadn't done it very well and was caught with his hand in the till.

Mr. Culpin didn't like skimmers but was known to be tolerant of those who turned a profit. A profit that they could share with Mr. Culpin. This he viewed as innovative financing. In his business, if you turned a profit and shared that money upwards then the means were justified by the ends. Steal and make a loss, however, and retribution was sure to find you.

From the moment the theft was discovered Robinson was watched. When he ran to a dodgy hotel in Soho, hoping the anonymity of London would hide him, he was watched. Shortly after he arrived the manager politely asked him to leave. He was watched when he went to ground in a flea-pit in Amsterdam where, not long after his arrival, he was once again asked to leave. He was watched as he arrived home in Southbourne hoping his friends would shelter him. It was then Mr. Culpin thought Mrs. Crosby and Mrs. Fitch would enjoy a trip to the seaside.

He had his men watch Robinson for a week before he contacted the ladies. Even Mr. Culpin didn't like to cause Mrs. Crosby and Mrs. Fitch trouble. He wanted to be reasonably sure Robinson was going to stay put and not cause the ladies any inconvenience by taking off to a new town before they'd executed their plans.

The day after Mr. Culpin had sent them the details of the job, Mrs. Crosby and Mrs. Fitch had spent a very pleasant day at the beach getting to know the area around the guest house where they'd been told that David Robinson was staying. After a morning exploring the area they had met an associate of Mr. Culpin's, drafted in from Yorkshire to keep an eye on Robinson. At his request, they had met in a rather shabby looking pub which the associate assured them served the best pie and chips in the neighborhood.

"Afternoon ladies. I'm John Rathbone. Mr. C said to give you the full gen on Robinson." He said around a mouthful of peas.

"Yes please," Mrs. Crosby replied, hoping he would perhaps stop eating while he did so.

"Well other than the occasional trip to the Spar on the corner for smokes and food he hasn't done much for as long as I've been here. He don't even go to the pub."

"He's expecting Mr. Culpin to come after him." Mrs. Crosby commented.

"Seems like."

"At least he's done the decent thing and kept away from his family, wouldn't want them getting caught up in this." Mrs. Fitch said, trying, as always, to see the best in everyone.

"No ma'am," Rathbone said, "She kicked him out as soon as she heard what he'd done. None of the cash he'd been skimming had gone anywhere near her and the kids, and I reckon she was sick of being saddled with such a loser. Plus, of course, she wouldn't want Mr. C thinking she were in on it and all."

"No, I can see that." Mrs. Fitch said. "So this is going to have to happen at the guest house. What's it like inside? The layout of the rooms I mean."

"Hallway from front door, leading to reception and stairs up on the left." He drew it out on a paper napkin, "Front room to the right, supposedly for guest use but I've never seen anyone in it. But it is the off season, it's just me and Robinson staying at the moment."

"That's good." Mrs. Crosby said. "How wide is the reception?"

"Not very." Rathbone answered. "There's a bit of a dog leg in the corridor as it goes round to the back, if you get me, and the counter runs around the corner but the front of it is just the width of the corridor."

"Good, good. And where's Robinson's room?"

"On the second floor. Up the stairs, third door on the left."

"Can you see the stairs from the front room?" Mrs. Fitch asked.

"No, they're further into the house. You have to be further up the hallway to see up the stairs."

"Creaky stairway is it?" asked Mrs. Crosby, who had guessed what her companion was planning.

"Not particularly." Rathbone answered, a little puzzled by the questions. "I've not noticed it."

"And you say you're the only other guest?" Mrs. Crosby pressed.

"That's right. Leastways I haven't seen or heard anyone else."

"I think that's everything we need." Mrs. Crosby said, "If he checks out or anyone else checks in before," she checked the date, "Thursday? Does that suit you Margaret?"

Mrs. Fitch nodded.

"If he checks out or anyone else checks in before Thursday, can you ask Mr. Culpin to let us know?" She took the paper napkin, folded it carefully and dropped it into her pocket. "Thank you very much Mr. Rathbone."

"Call me John," Rathbone said. "You're Mr. C's advance team are you? Reporting back to the boss?"

"Oh dear me no." Mrs. Fitch said brightly, "Well good day dear. Adele? Shall we?"

The two ladies left the pub and walked back down to the beach and along the front.

"The light sponge maneuver?" Mrs. Crosby asked.
"The light sponge maneuver." Mrs. Fitch agreed.

They couldn't put their plan in to action immediately, the eponymous cake needed baking first and they hadn't any equipment with them, so they had spent the rest of the day enjoying the sea air and talking over their options, trying to make the most of the small time available to them to put the plan together.

Ordinarily Mrs. Crosby and Mrs. Fitch liked to spend at least a month setting up a job like this. Careful planning was key in being able to get in, do the job and get out again without notice. Especially when they had to allow for Mrs. Fitch's occasionally difficult hip. But for dear Mr. Culpin, a very old friend and business associate, they had been willing to take on a rush job.

Now, just three days later, they were ready. They settled their bill at the teashop and stepped out onto the promenade where it was still drizzling.

"It is a shame about this weather." Mrs. Fitch commented as they walked down one of the back streets heading towards the guest house where David Robinson was still staying. "Oh well, we shall be able to get some doughnuts for the journey home even if it doesn't turn out to be much of a day out."

"Oh, careful Margaret," Mrs. Crosby said as they reached the guest house, "These steps are rather treacherous. Give me your arm. Now, let's get this done shall we?" she asked as Mrs. Fitch opened the front door and checked that the hallway was clear.

Mrs. Fitch rang the bell at the reception desk while Mrs. Crosby snuck into the front room from where she would be able to get to the stairs, with luck, without being seen once Mrs. Fitch had the manager distracted. Mrs. Crosby looked around the room. This really was a seedy place, she thought. The carpets were worn through in most places, which was a blessing from Mrs. Crosby's point of view as the pattern was hideous and, with a different carpet in each of the visible rooms, quite migraine-inducing. There was a faint smell of rot coming from somewhere. Mrs. Crosby decided she really did not want to know where.

An obese man with greasy hair plastered over a bald pate came to the front desk.

"Help you Miss?"

"I do hope so," said Mrs. Fitch in her best chatty old lady manner, "I'm a little lost. I was looking for the Edelweiss Tea Rooms and I must have taken a wrong turn somewhere. I'm sixty-eight you know," she said brightly. "I was planning to come down with my friend, and she's much better at navigating than I am but she was taken ill poor dear. The train tickets were all booked and I was so looking forward to a day at the seaside I thought I'd come down anyway." Mrs. Fitch continued to chat away, while Mrs. Crosby waited. The light sponge maneuver couldn't be rushed.

"Ooh, listen to me prattle on. I am sorry for taking up so much of your time. I have this little map here." Mrs. Fitch started rummaging in her large bag, brought along for just this purpose. "Oh it's in here somewhere, I know it is. Here, have one of these while I'm ferreting." she said, handing the man a plastic container filled with slices of cake. "They're slices of my Lemon Drizzle cake. I've won prizes for them. No, please, help yourself. You've been so kind letting me chatter on this way." The edges of the plastic lid had been worn down, making it very difficult to grasp the lid and open the box. As the dreadful man was focused on trying to open the box and Mrs. Fitch opened up her large tourist's map of Southbourne, Mrs. Crosby snuck carefully past and up to the first floor.

Fifteen minutes later Mrs. Fitch heard a toilet flushing, a noise that the manager of the guest house ignored as the usual sounds of guests upstairs but that Mrs. Fitch knew to be the sign that David Robinson was now dead. Time to move on to the second phase of the light sponge maneuver.

"You wouldn't have any tea in the house would you dear? Cake like this goes down so much nicer with a spot of tea and I'm absolutely parched after my journey down here."

Mrs. Fitch's lemon drizzle cake had worked its usual wonders and she and the odious man were sat in the hotel's front room with the box of cake slices in front of them. She had been listening to him talk about the boxing match he had been to the night before, making the right encouraging noises so that it sounded like she was fascinated with his story. People, she had found, were always happy to chat away to a receptive ear. It helped that she was genuinely interested in people, although this fellow and his revolting guest house were pushing even the limits of her interest.

"Of course Mrs. Fitch. I'm sorry, I should have offered before. Can't have cake without tea now can we?" he laughed and lumbered out of the front room and towards the back of the house to the kitchen.

Mrs. Crosby nodded to Mrs. Fitch as she quickly moved through the entrance hall and out of the front door, marveling at Mrs. Fitch's ability to get seemingly anyone to sit down and talk over a slice of cake. It was a talent that was just as important to their past and future successes as her own ability to kill people quietly and with a minimum of fuss and mess. They were a good team.

Thirty minutes later Mrs. Fitch left the company of the man at the guest house and joined Mrs. Crosby back on the promenade. Mrs. Crosby had been sitting on one of the benches watching the sea, something old people are expected to do at the seaside. No one batted an eye as they passed her; being old really was the best cover in the world.

"All done, Adele?"

"All done." Mrs. Crosby replied, "And by the state of the rest of that guest house, I don't believe anyone will find his body until the rent comes due." She stood up from the bench, "Now I believe something was said about doughnuts."

"Oh yes." agreed Mrs. Fitch, "And now that business is out of the way, we can get on to more important matters. What are you planning to enter in the cake competition this year?"

"I haven't quite decided yet," Mrs. Crosby confided to her friend, "I'm torn between a classic Victoria sponge and a new recipe I found for a rich dark ginger cake."

"Ooh, that sounds nice. I bet it would be lovely with a bit of cheese. I'm thinking of entering an apple and cinnamon cake. Do you remember I brought it to Hester's garden party last month?"

Mrs. Crosby and Mrs. Fitch walked out, arm in arm, down the promenade towards the doughnut stall, looking like nothing more than a couple of old ladies out for the day, with little going on in their lives aside from lady's meetings, bingo and knitting.

But to those in the know, they were the best contract killers currently working in the United Kingdom and, for the right price, occasionally abroad, although Mrs. Fitch didn't care so much for long haul flights these days. Just two old ladies filling the days of retirement as best they could.

Caroline Cormack *lives and works in London, UK, and, unlike most of the city's commuters, she is really looking forward to the London 2012 Olympics. What an excellent backdrop for a crime story! Caroline has been writing short stories and plays since she was a teenager. Having recently started to submit stories to magazines, The Light Sponge Maneuver is her first published story. Caroline can be found on Twitter as @bookclubdropout.*

COLD CALL

Scott Taylor

Hank stepped out of the shower and wiped the fog from the mirror, his own bloodshot eyes stared back at him. He shaved with greater care than normal, making faces to pull the skin tight while the razor scraped through the stubble. After rinsing his razor and toweling off, he splashed some Aqua Velva out into his palm, then slapped it onto the raw skin. The clean smell stung his nostrils.

Running a comb through his hair, he tamed the most unruly cowlicks with a dab of Brylcream. Satisfied with the results, he trudged to his bedroom, and tore the plastic dry cleaner's bag off his best black suit.

The funeral suit.

He was tying the laces on his Florsheims when the phone rang. The noise startled him, and he snapped a lace clean off.

"Shit."

He looked at the phone for confirmation, and it rang again. Who would be calling today? Now? Another ring, the jangling bell unnerved Hank and he snatched up the receiver to avoid hearing it split the silence again. He listened to the hiss on the line a moment before speaking.

"Hello?"

"Hello, is this Hank Wade?"

"Yes." Hank squeezed the handset. It felt greasy in his grip.

"Detective Hank Wade, homicide division, Cleveland P.D.?" The caller was cordial, but impersonal. Like someone selling something.

"Yeah… listen, it's not a real good time right now." Hank wondered if he had another shoelace in his sock drawer.

"I can understand that, Detective Wade. I am aware that you are on your way to witness a murder, but there is something you need to know."

Witness a murder? Okay, so it was a reporter, or one of those human rights people. "I am on my way to witness the *execution* of a very bad man." Time for the canned speech. "While I am aware that not everyone agrees with capital punishment, it is the law of the land. My job is simply to enforce the laws. If you have a problem with the death penalty, you need to take it up with your legislator."

A chuckle, cold and hard made Hank pull the earpiece away in shock. When he put it back to his ear the voice was mid sentence. "…certainly don't have a problem with murder, either sanctioned by the state or otherwise."

"Okay, whatever. Does this call have a point?" Hank leaned over the mirror on his bureau, tugging at the knot in his tie with his free hand.

"I just wanted to welcome you to the club."

"This isn't my first execution. I've had men put down before. Goes with the job."

"Petty crooks with handguns. Husbands crazed by jealousy. Men driven by greed to plot against other men. Those aren't quite the same animal as the one you're dealing with tonight."

"Meaning?"

"I'm sure it gets to you sometimes, Detective, watching an execution that you helped bring about. Especially hard when the guy getting juiced is some poor jerk who just got caught up in the wrong circumstances. But this one is different. A serial killer, a real honest to goodness psycho." The voice on the other end of the line was like a steel wheels on rails. Hank's knuckles ached, and he realized that he was clenching the coiled cord that led to the handset.

"Must be a good feeling," the voice continued, "knowing that this one is different than any of those previous executions. This one is… righteous."

"Geoffrey Allen Sadler deserves to die. I don't feel bad about it, but that doesn't mean I feel good about it, either." But Hank knew the caller was right.

Righteous. After all of the gruesome discoveries of the past several months, after the next of kin notifications, the courtroom testimonies and the anger and frustration, why not allow himself the luxury of righteousness? Especially on this night of closure.

"Who is this?" It amazed Hank that it did not occur to him until this moment to ask the obvious question.

"That is an excellent question, Hank. First class police work." Another ice cold chuckle. "I'm the man you were looking for all those months. The man you woke up in the middle of the night thinking about. I'm the Decapitator."

Hank's jaw was clenched tight. "No. Geoffrey Sadler is the man responsible for those crimes. And he is going to pay for them at midnight tonight."

"I almost wish for your sake that could be true. No, Detective, Geoffrey was a patsy. I set him up to take the fall for what I did."

"Okay, that's bull. If this is some kind of eleventh hour stunt to get Sadler a stay…"

"Around her hair, she wore a yellow ribbon… " the voice cooed in a sing-song. "That's something you didn't release to the papers isn't it, Hank?"

A lock of hair from each victim, bound with a yellow ribbon had been mailed to the police station after every headless corpse had been discovered. The heads had all been found buried in Sadler's vegetable patch.

"Sadler could have told you about the hair. We caught the guy, he was tried, convicted, and now he's gonna pay. Simple as that."

"Of course he's going to pay. How could you stop the execution now, even if you wanted to? Whom would you call? Your Chief? The D.A.? The Governor? And what could you say to convince them? How to explain that after months of solid police work, a mound of evidence, a jury conviction and two appeals, you received a phone call that gave you the willies?"

It was Hank's turn to chuckle. "As if a phone call from some dirtbag pal of Sadler's would be enough to save his skin."

"Don't get nasty. It's unnecessary and unflattering. I don't want the execution called off any more than you do. Relax, Hank. Like I said, Sadler is my fall guy, and I'm gonna let him fall. And you don't have to worry about anymore inconvenient headless corpses surfacing, or any more locks of hair in ribbons showing up. I've packed up and left town. As far as anyone needs know, you got your man."

"You're damn right I got my man. Sadler told you about the hair, and you thought you'd just call me and mess with-"

"But I'm going to tell you something else, Hank. Something that Geoffrey Sadler couldn't possibly have told me. I'm going to tell you the future."

"Like how I'm gonna hang up on your ass in about three seconds?"

"If you were going to hang up, you would have done it already. Here's my prediction; in less than a week, police in Tucson, Arizona will find the first of several bodies. They will all bear the same disfigurement, namely the ring finger will be severed from each and a number will be carved into their chests. After a twelve month investigation, Tucson's finest will arrest the culprit, who will be tried, convicted and sentenced to die. On the eve of that man's execution, the arresting officer will get a call from me."

"To what end?"

"Well...here's something you can do, that will be fun for you." The voice on the line was more animated now; the caller was having a good time. "Call up Detective William Banks in Fresno, California. He caught the Westside Sniper. Then call Jimbo Reese, in Chigaco. He brought down the Miracle Man. Yulee Flint of the Texas Rangers caught the guy the papers were calling Able."

"What are you talking about?" Hank's voice came out half an octave higher that he expected it to.

"All members of your club, Detective Wade. All caught their men red-handed. Had them tried in a court of law, and sentenced to death. And on the eve of each of those executions, they received a call from me."

"And you confessed to the crimes committed by the other men." Hank almost hung up the phone, *knew* he should hang up the phone, but something held him frozen, gripping the handset. "Nice little game you've got worked out, but I don't feel like playing."

"You have already played, and lost. Tonight at midnight, Geoffrey Allen Sadler will be put to death. And he will become my next victim, murdered by remote control. I only regret that I can't be there to see it, I'll have to read about it in the papers tomorrow morning."

A paralyzing dread was crawling out of Hank's gut, climbing his ribcage, prickling the base of his skull. "Why?" It was pathetic and weak, but it was all Hank could muster.

"I suppose this is the place where I say something ominous, like *'Look on every one that is proud, and bring him low; and tread down the wicked in their place...'* But, the truth is, I just like listening to virtuous pricks like you squirm as the curtain is slowly drawn back, and you realize that you are my accomplice.

"It amuses me that I can hear your throat tighten when you realize that every clue you uncovered over the past few months was planted, every step you took closer to your suspect was another step closer to my victim. I delight in the silence on the other end of the line when you grasp that in a couple of hours, you will have to sit and look into the eyes of an innocent man while he is strapped down, and murdered. Murdered by my will and your compliance.

"Are you still with me, Detective?"

Hank couldn't remember sinking slowly to the floor, his back sliding down the wall, but that's where he found himself sitting, receiver still clamped to his ear. His mouth moved, but no sound came out.

"Thank you, Detective Wade, you've been more than helpful."

Click.

Scott Taylor *writes words, linked into sentences that form pictures in your brain.*

SUNSET RAILROAD TRESTLE CASCO BAY *by Bradley Roland*

Bradley Roland *is an engineer working for the Portland Public Works Department. He lives in Portland, Maine with his family. He an avid biker and photographer.*

Risk Factor

Ken Doyle

She pours the Scotch into her glass, savoring the rich, peaty aroma. The golden liquid is the only color evident in the uniform grayness of her world. Outside the window, snowflakes swirl and collect in clusters, partly obscuring her view of the street below. She watches the fuzzy figures moving, like a monochrome herd of cattle, down the broad sidewalk of Westland Avenue. With a collective purpose, they head for Symphony Hall. Most of them have their collars turned up, but every now and then, she catches a glimpse of a man's lifeless tie, or a woman's dull pearls. The wind sings a lament outside her window, and she bows her head for a moment.

Muffled honking intrudes on her thoughts. An eCar tries to shoehorn itself into a parking space. It is the only break in the gray line of eCars that stretches along the street, as far as she can see.

She sighs, and turns her gaze from the window. Her spartan studio apartment offers little comfort. The two bow-backed chairs, the couch with its familiar rip down the side, the digiframe of her mother that hangs above the couch—she tries to remember how they looked in color. Especially her mother. Young, vibrant, a picture of health. It's good to see her that way. Before the cancer came back, and spread to her bones.

She reaches into her purse for her iPhone. She hesitates, then swipes a finger across the glossy screen.

The color started fading the day before. She had problems sleeping again, and a quick text to her doctor was all it took. Within a few minutes, a texted response from the pharmacy informed her that the prescription was ready. The KwikDrug was just across the street, nestled between a Stop-N-Go and an all-night Laundromat. Its white mortar and pestle blinked fiercely at her as she made her way down the crumbling stairs of the converted brownstone.

She saw the sign by the counter where she picked up her prescription. It shouted, in bold red letters: *Free Genome Sequencing: Results While You Wait!* The instrument itself looked far too small to sequence an entire genome, though of course she had no idea how big a genome was supposed to be. Vague memories of high-school biology surfaced, something about twenty-three pairs of chromosomes...

"Is that really free?" she asked the pharmacist.

He smiled. "As the sign says, for a limited time only. KwikDrug is the first chain of drugstores in the country to introduce these machines. They're made by iBio, you know." His chest looked like it would burst through his white coat.

She tried to look impressed. He went on, explaining how the sequencing chemistry was a major breakthrough, and that the technology had lowered the cost of sequencing the human genome to less than $100. It really didn't matter to her, as long as it was free.

"What do I have to do? Will it hurt?" Visions of huge needles clouded her eyes.

His eyes twinkled. "Not at all." He reached over the counter and pressed a button on the machine. She watched as it hummed and the screen began flashing messages. He handed her a plastic tube, no bigger than a pen.

"When you're ready," he said, "just open the tube, and swab the inside of your cheek. Then insert the swab into this slot, here." He pointed at a penny-sized indentation. A green glow throbbed around its edge, waiting for her.

"The sign said 'While you wait.' How long does it really take?"

The pharmacist shrugged. "Less than thirty minutes for the sequencing run." He looked at the iPhone clasped in her left hand. "If you prefer, we can get the report sent directly to your iPhone in a couple of hours. I should advise you, though, that we recommend professional genetic counseling when you receive the results. The report can be confusing, and..."

She raised a hand. "Let's get this over with."

She swallowed, fighting back a sudden wave of panic. She opened the plastic tube, removed the swab, and put it into her mouth. Just like a toothbrush. It felt like one too, as she twirled it. She inserted the tip of the swab into the machine, and watched as it was sucked in the rest of the way. The machine acknowledged her efforts in a nasal but clear voice. She filled out the rest of the information on the screen. Without looking back at the pharmacist, she turned and left the store. She made her way back to the apartment in a daze.

Her iPhone brings a chilling dose of reality. She flicks down the list, to the message that changed everything. Maybe if she reads it again...

DPC4 MSH2 MSH6 The strange acronyms float before her eyes like the snowflakes outside. Genes implicated in breast cancer. Of course, her last checkup was fine, and her doctor had said she'd never been healthier. Aside from the occasional restless night, that is.

Her eyes scroll past the summary of risk factors and down to the disclaimer, in a font so small she has to squint to read it. Something about genetic counseling, your mileage may vary, past performance is no guarantee of future results, caveat emptor...

With a sigh, she puts the iPhone down on the insipid kitchen counter top. She removes a spoon from a drawer. With a flick of her wrist, she empties the bottle of pills onto the counter. She mashes them with the spoon, and then scoops the powder into her Scotch.

A brilliant kaleidoscope of color explodes across her vision, as the liquid burns a path down her throat.

Ken Doyle *published his first short story at the age of thirteen. His early work appeared in an anthology of Indian science fiction, "It Happened Tomorrow." Ken has been writing and editing nonfiction professionally since 1995, specializing in science and technology. He has authored regular technology columns for local publications, including the* Fitchburg Star *and the* Capital Region Business Journal, *as well as online content for* Yahoo Content Network. *By day, Ken is employed as a marketing professional at a biotech company in Madison, Wisconsin. He is working on his first young adult science fiction novel.*

AUTOPORN CACHE

Sara Kate Ellis

It's one lousy dry afternoon in Corona Del Mar, and I'm trying to read Popular Mechanics. My sister and grandpa are yelling, and I can only focus on the ads. Sloop John B is on the AM, all muddy water rushing through a player piano, and my sister's pulling her hair out because there's a quarter less gas in the tank and she's sure grandpa took the keys again. He's not supposed to drive. He's real forgetful and his reflexes are slowing.

"That's a hundred bucks you just wasted acting like some petulant kid," she says. "How are we going to get that back?"

We use the car maybe once a month for emergency errands, or when we just get so cooped up that we want to kill each other. The rest of the time it's a carpool or the big diesel rumblers that bus me into the canyon and back on school days.

My eyes dart from the magazine to the embrasure leading into the kitchen. Grandpa's opening and closing his mouth like a puppet, trying to clench his jaw, but his teeth don't line up.

"I didn't do anything." He jerks a ragged hand toward a cookie jar, jammed full of dried out pens and receipts. "You want your damn keys, they're right there."

My sister blows a strand of sweaty hair out of her face, and turns back to see her key ring where he says it is, propped up on the counter like a piece of rusty fruit.

"This is the last time," she says.

"It ain't even the first."

When Dad died, we tried out a home for a year, but it cost too much, so here he is. I'm supposed to keep an eye on him when my sister's out, but there was a lockdown at school due to air quality, and I got home late. Now she's rushing around the house, trying to get ready for her second shift at a corrections facility in Carlsbad.

She drops her keys into her purse and snaps it shut. "You just keep it up. Pretty soon they'll toss you in the clink for stunts like that."

"Clink?" He says it like it sounds funny.

Even though she got grandpa's license revoked, there's little chance he'll be pulled over until the law goes into effect, when anyone over sixty-five is banned from operating a motor vehicle. My government teacher Mr. Tran calls it chicken shit, says they're too scared to take on the big polluters, so they go kick up a fit about aging boomers and rising accident rates.

"Too little, too late," he says. He likes to say that a lot.

Grandpa comes into the living room, lowering himself into a battered green easy chair with cigarette burns in one of the arms. He's wheezing, which is probably how my sister sniffed him out, and I wonder if that's how smokers used to sound. I turn on my side and try to focus on the article, but I can still see that shamed, glassy smile from the corner of my eye.

"Whatcha got there, Suze?" he asks.

Reluctantly, I sit up, swinging my legs off the sofa to give him space. "One of Dad's. I just found it out in the garage."

The just is for his benefit. He's already been through Dad's things because there were other magazines and old movies that started going missing right after he moved in. The ones I'd really been looking for. Like most autoporn, they're worth money; some of them are even illegal, but I don't care about that. It's the women. Their bodies aren't swaddled in filterweave and you can see their skin, their necks and shoulders, their legs.

"That's a Corvette," grandpa says. "I used to drive one of those." He points to one all needle-nosed and sleek, like some kind of sea creature that might slip out of the wet sand and slice you right in half.

"No you didn't," my sister yells from upstairs.

Outside the all clear sounds, which means the wind has picked up enough to let us go out if need be. No one ever does. When I was little, there was a group of kids who played basketball at an old hoop in the cul-de-sac, but I haven't seen anyone hanging around there in years except cats.

"That's a C6, could get up to two hundred and five miles per hour."

He presses a gnarled thumb over another car, this time red, and I nod, wondering why they'd make something go that fast if it was already against the law.

"You okay for food?" my sister yells. Her ride will be pulling up any minute, and I yell back a "Yeah," but I'm getting hungry and thinking I don't want to eat the leftovers. Last night she made some peppery soup that tasted like the air outside.

"I know where one is," grandpa whispers. "Want to see the real thing?"

"Can we pick up Chinese?" I'm only half serious. Right now he reminds me of this scrawny kid one class below me, the one who lies all the time and gets beat up.

"I do," he says.

I shrug. There's no way he's getting those keys back.

"Suze," he smiles, his voice raspy with possibility. "I know where she keeps the spare set."

Grandpa says the sky wasn't brown when he was my age. At night there was just enough smog to turn it pink. My sister can remember it, too, but I'd been born late, right after she left for college.

We zigzag slowly down what's left of the old Pacific Coast Highway, and the shoreline against the dark looks like a long strip of fat on a pork chop. I should be watching grandpa's driving, but it beats me how anyone could get in a wreck at this speed. He'll die of old age before we do that.

"What I told you back at the house," he says. "It's one hundred percent true."

"About what?"

"The Corvette. It was a beaut too. Really hurt when it got stolen."

He slows down as we approach a checkpoint, nothing serious along this strip. Not like the cops with their smog guns parked up and down the 405.

"What color was it?"

"Orange, red. I don't remember." For a second, his smile disappears, as if he's left the stove on back home. Then he picks up, continues as if the whole thing is just occurring to him in real time. "When that guy stole it, I had to go chasin' him all over the country. Spent a whole summer doin' just that."

"You go to New York?"

"I think so," he says. "I think I did. And Texas."

There's a long silence before the guards wave us past the checkpoint. They're looking for gas hogs and speed racer types, not my sister's old Honda. The traffic is finally thinning out, fewer rumblers and grassoline scooters and more of those fancy foreign hybrids with state-of-the-art air filters and double thick safety glass. Grandpa waves his hand at them dismissively.

"You didn't need all that then. Sun was shining all the time. You could go out in it as long as you liked. Take your dog out for a walk on the beach and watch him roll in dead birds. I met a girl who helped me out. Name was…name escapes me, but she drove me all over hell and back until we found her. The car, I mean."

"Was she pretty?"

He frowns before answering. "The car?"

"No."

I wonder if my sudden queasiness is because we're slaloming at a faster pace. Rapid coastal erosion has turned this once gentle ramble into a patchwork of crisscrossing stitches, swerving inland then sea-ward then back like some great cement scar.

Grandpa slows before turning abruptly off the highway onto a steep and winding path that takes us through an abandoned development. People used to live here, I think. People used to think they wouldn't fall in, and I reel back in my seat as we barrel headlong down the hill over pavement that feels more like clay. I yell for him to stop, but that look on his face is wild, almost happy.

We're angled almost straight down, the reeds and overgrowth streaking the sides of the car with a grimy war paint, as we stagger to a halt before an ancient, weatherworn sign: "Caution. Road Closed Permanently due to Erosion."

I can still feel my heart jounce. Grandpa's hunched over the dash, as if trying to get a last glimpse of a thrill that's now slipping away.

"You still alive?" I loosen my hand from the door handle now slick with sweat.

He coughs out a chuckle as I hand him a sheet of filterweave, wrapping my own carefully around my nose and mouth, tucking it behind my ears the way Dad taught me when the clouds first crossed the sea. He used to weave it through his fingers, play all sorts of games.

"This stuff," he'd say. "It's like that chicken egg problem, only very, very stupid. Bunch of politicos got people all riled up, said *they* were going to embargo our oil, wrap our women up in gunnysacks, so we started a bunch of wars until the wells were on fire, and the ash got so bad we're all wrapped up now. What do you think, Suze? That funny or what?"

My filterweave is downy and smells like mint. We've gotten ours mixed up, and Grandpa's got the strawberry chew, a girly smell, but he doesn't seem to care. When we step outside, the air is surprisingly clear, and I'm tempted to lift the cloth and let some of its salty mist on my tongue, but I hear a kick and juddering sound. Grandpa is laughing, standing over the caution sign, now leaning at a sharp angle toward the ground. He's acting just like my sister said, a petulant kid. "Tell us somethin' we don't know," he says.

I spot the rim of a guardrail that once might have protected us peeking out between the rocks and tufts of reed grass like a row of dirty teeth. Around us, the remaining houses stand vigilant against the sandy churn below, some sagging backward, rearing back in shock.

I wonder if Grandpa wants to follow suit, to step off the cliff into some irretrievable past. Instead, he sits down and pats the sand beside him. I make my way over, careful to stay a good four feet from the brink.

"I thought we were going to see a car."

He takes a thin flashlight from his pocket and aims it at the water below. I can see little, just the white foam of the waves, a few jagged shadows poking their noses out of the water like sharks responding to the beam.

"It's down there."

"What?"

"The car. This kid I was mad at, name escapes me. He went right down into the water."

I wonder how that could have happened if the shore was farther out, but I don't say anything. The wind's picked up and it's getting cold. I want to get my food and get back.

"I was new at school see, and this kid, forgot his name. He didn't like me. Thought I was moving in on his girl, so he said 'Hey Joe, how about a game of chicken?'"

That last word hits my stomach and I start to worry that he's forgetting our deal. I want to get orange chicken if we ever get out of here. Mr. Tran calls it "fake ethnic food," but it's a favorite and we don't get it very often.

"The idea is that the coward, the chicken, they go speeding toward the cliff. Guy who gets closest to the edge wins, only this kid, he couldn't stop. Went right over. He's still down there."

"You go to jail?" I ask, but the thing is, I know he's lying. Grandpa lies a lot, but it never sounds like he is, because when he talks, it comes out of him all desperate, like he's passing on bits of his own history and he'll disappear if we don't hear him out. The best thing I can do is humor him. Make him feel good. Make him hurry.

"No. We just took off out of there, bunch of scared kids, and the police asked around, but they put it down to an accident. I don't know why I remember this so well. I'm forgettin' everything else these days."

But it's all still there. When he's out of the house, I can go through his things, find the magazines he took, along with Dad's movie collection, and one of them, I know, will have some cocky kid who drives off a cliff because he can't open the door in time. It always turns out this way. That two-lane blacktop he likes to talk about wasn't his to begin with; he's just doing his best to get it back.

When we get to the car, he hands me the keys.

"There's no way." I point to the front fender, just a few inches short of the abyss. "Besides, I'm not allowed."

"Neither am I," he says. "But there's a difference now. You ain't going to be."

He's right. I've got five more years until I can get behind the wheel, and by then the rules will be so tight I probably won't get the chance. But I do know how. I've watched the movies, read the manuals, practiced steering and braking in the driveway.

"Come on, Suze," he says. "I can take it back up the hill first if you're..."

"Chicken? Yeah, I kind of am."

But I do say yes, because I know what he's giving up: one last look at a time where we could do almost anything we wanted, use up what we wanted, and the hell with the rest. This ride will be my first and last. And that's how I can know him, know how his world worked, rushing from start to finish, faster and faster until the end was the only thing left, and the middle?

Some old movie with a Corvette and a pretty girl.

Sara Kate Ellis *lives in Tokyo where she is a master of seat nabbing during crowded commutes. Her stories have appeared in* Allegory, Brain Harvest *and* The Red Penny Papers. *She is a 2011 Lambda Fellow in Genre Fiction.*

The Clog

Wesley Dylan Gray

Fingers slide into the drain,
Hot, moist, and steaming.
Open hole accepting
To my tender violations.

Nails scrape to separate,
Matted hair from steel.
Pull the clog — it will not budge.
Yank the hair — the slimy tangles.

The hole now parting, morphing, dilating;
It stretches and a head emerges.
As a boatman tugging line,
I'm hand over hand, and heaving.

I stand clenching clog;
The flesh blue-gay with odor,
Lifted from the darkness —
A body dripping, beaded up in drops.

As an author of dark fiction and poetry, Wesley Dylan Gray *is a writer who is difficult to classify. With his words he attempts to exude a disposition of resplendent contrast, writing things of darkness and light, things both beautiful and grotesque. Such writings can be found in a variety of magazines and anthologies. He resides in Florida with his wife and daughter. Discover more at the author's website: www.wesleydylangray.com.*

SERVICE

Gary Campbell

Even though Sheri had the car I still got home long before she--they--did.

"Watch your step," the bus said in its big avuncular voice as I wrestled my packages out the door. There was the bag from the hardware store, the large box, and the longer item I'd wrapped to hide its shape. When I got inside, I unwrapped it and slid it under the bed. The box held a flat black rectangle about two feet square and a couple inches thick, with a power cord. It was an industrial-strength degausser, the kind they use to erase big hard drives. I spent some time rigging a handle for it with duct tape and strapping from the hardware store. Then I stashed it in the garage, loaded my nail gun with a brand-new 16d clip, and settled down to wait. I'd been doing a lot of waiting lately. That didn't make me any better at it.

I bounced around a house which had once been described as gracious but was actually just too big for two people. I wound up on a chair in the bedroom, nodding already, wanting to sleep but not in--I almost said "our" bed. It had been such a long day. So much had happened. It all got jumbled up, confused...

Everything would have been fine if she just hadn't started fucking the car. I should have known something was up when she dumped our friendly old Ford Humungous for that low-slung Italian job: Testaroni. She started coming home late, that new-car smell about her, exhaust fumes on her breath.

I went to one of those love-sting places; they only served humans. I hired a detective who wound up laughing in my face. Finally, I found Auto-Erotic, a small agency whose founder's husband had dumped her for a Corvette.

Kiki Mallow was fortyish, brunette, hardly unattractive, though she was starting to show the effects of many hours spent sitting in cars at stakeouts eating junk food. She picked me up this morning, right after Sheri and her greasy squeeze had tooled off into the haze.

"Ooh, you look so good," her Porsche said as I slid into its leather seat. "You've lost weight. Your butt's so small I can hardly tell any-one's sitting on me."

Mallow's hand flicked out and hit a button. "Sorry," she said. "I for-got to turn off the ego boost. Want a massage?"

"What?"

"The seat vibrates; gives you a massage."

"Uh, no."

There was no mystery about where Sheri was going. The Ziggurat is a sort of automotive ossuary, where lifeless cars lay on slabs waiting to be re-animated at the end of the day. It's webbed with moving walk-ways. The cars sit, and the people move.

We pulled in behind a column across from Sheri's reserved spot. There was Testaroni, crouching on Sheri's square, his tires touching her name, a self-satisfied smirk on his perfect grille.

We settled down to wait. Have I said this before?

"I can't stand it anymore."

"Relax, Steele," Mallow said. "Have a Twinkie."

"Are you all right?" the car purred. "Anything I can do?" The seat trembled in anticipation.

I cracked the door. "I've got to stretch my legs."

"We've only been here five minutes."

It was better out of the car. I took a few steps, vaguely in the direc-tion of Testaroni.

"Don't get too close," Mallow warned; no need. I knew exactly the limits of his motion sensors. I'd spent hours staring at him in the gar-age, wondering. Was it only a fling, or could he give Sheri something I couldn't?

I angled to get behind him, ducking from column to column to column . . . they're all alike aren't they? Maybe there's only one, and it's moving while I walk in place. It's so hard to tell. I had a better sense of direction before I quit taking those pills.

Hours later, when I found them again, they were having a heart-to-heart. Mallow was sobbing, baring her hurts. The car was stroking her, being supportive, sounding like it really understood. I didn't want to intrude.

It was dark before I found the spot again. Mallow was gone, but not Testaroni. He wasn't quiet either.

I took a chance, dropping and crawling toward him. Sure enough, his motion sensors were off. The way he was rocking they'd have to be. I crept closer, put my ear to the door, glanced briefly in the window. Sheri was there, leaning back, squealing like she did in bed. Testaroni was vibrating for all he was worth, saying, 'oh baby you're so hot. That's it, do it again yeah, yeah, yeah' and it was then that I knew what I had to do.

I had to murder the car.

Hitting the floor woke me up. What was--yes! A car door. They were home.

I dived into bed and pretended to sleep. It was the worst waiting of the day. Sheri was a long time in the bathroom, then she tossed and turned in a sweaty post-coital sort of way. At long last, when I was sure she was finally asleep, I reached under the bed for the axe. It had a yellow fiberglass handle advertised as unbreakable. We'd see.

I spent a long time feeling the blade and studying Sheri's throat. When she moved there was a glint of metal. It was the chain I'd got her when we were first married. It was threaded with a tiny golden nut, a private joke between us. We were so nuts about each other we started calling ourselves Mr. and Mrs. Nut.

She still loved me. It wasn't her fault. We were both victims. I knew who was *really* to blame, and he was waiting for me downstairs.

Testaroni woke to the sound of nails being shot into his tires.

"Back off," he warned. "You are too close to the vehicle."

"Not this time, asshole," I growled, and squeezed the trigger. The gun spit 16d galvanized slugs, a neat circle of them, right through the windshield.

His flat tires flopped as he came right at me. I dived at his windshield, crashed through, stuck halfway in. Close enough. I groped under his dash.

Testaroni accelerated, braked, backed, accelerated. My chest was slick with blood, but all I felt was cold.

Finally, I found what I was groping for. I pulled the hood release. That really scared him. He yawed wildly, left and right. As he shook me off my foot snagged a hose. Coolant spewed electric-green. His alarm screamed. Or maybe it was mine.

He nearly took me out with a vicious swerve. I dodged, rolled, came up holding the de-gausser.

When he lunged again I climbed up under his hood. I tore off his computer cover, slammed the de-gausser right up against his chips, and squeezed.

"Oh baby you're so hot," he whimpered. His engine stalled. Testaroni shuddered, gave a last gasp of exhaust, and died.

Then the axe. I shattered his grille, punched out his windows, and hacked off both his doors. Then I went to work on his engine. Sometime during the process, I looked up.

Sheri cracked a wicked grin.

"I didn't know you had it in you," she said, and on her face was pure lust.

I took her, right there on the engine block of her disemboweled lover, with wires tangled like guts and Sheri screaming like a 12-cylinder wide open, with blood running and oil bubbling and hydraulic fluid spurting and my piston pumping over and over...

Gary Campbell *was born on the planet Earth. At least he thinks it's Earth. At any rate he's fairly certain it's covered with earth.*

After interminably irritating his parents and teachers, Gary attended the Antediluvian Institute of Technology. There he devised several plausible mathematical explanations for how many angels can dance on the head of a pin. he was finally granted a degree, his professors concluding that was the most effective way to get rid of him.

Hard-won (sort of) physics degree in hand, Gary promptly proceeded to ignore his chosen field. He built TV studios and directed television shows. He's written plays, some of which were produced, and screenplays, none of which were produced (too few explosions and naked women.) He once starred in a no-budget science fiction movie which fortunately has now vanished from this and every other planet. He works at a well-known film school in an engineering capacity.

He currently lives on Earth. At least he thinks it's earth

Interrogate My Heart Instead

Elaheh Steinke

To my mom.
To each and every person who fought for freedom.

He has forgotten that he used to exist and that he used to love him. He doesn't even think about him while taking a shower. They have told him that if he stabs people in the chest, or hits them in the streets of his own hometown, he would make God happy.

He has forgotten that he once wanted to see a lawyer to get his right to marry him. He has forgotten that blonde guys used to turn him on and he was the only brunette he ever wanted to be with. He was an exception, but now he's just like anyone who's been captured because of protesting for "Human Value".

He's looking for something that he'd never find: The Meaning of His Life. He can't recall his past. He can't even recall yesterday's interrogations, innocent faces, shattered minds of young boys and girls in the room. What has he done! How many boys and girls he must have had screwed, physically and mentally.

She's strong, beautiful even with the blindfold on, held together and ready. He doesn't like the last part.

Ready.

Readiness makes it hard to get over a genius mind. She won't suffer, she won't scream, she wouldn't beg. He doesn't like it. He has seen hundreds of young girls in the torture room. They all expect to be saved; saved by a call, a miracle, saved by God. But this one, this girl, she's ready for everything to happen. The blindfold has made her even scarier.

Her indifferent smile, her crossed hands that have hugged her breasts intimidates him. He wears his invisible mask and walks towards her. She won't get out of here. That smile shouldn't be seen outside these walls.

He wakes up from a dreamless sleep. It is the weekend but he has bones to crush, smiles to make disappear, lives to get. It's a new day, it's a new dawn, and he's gonna be a step closer to Heaven and God.

He has forgotten that he couldn't even think about fucking girls. He could like them, hate them, love them but he couldn't fall in love with any. He couldn't even manage to *try* to sleep with any. Ali was his first and he was meant to be the last one. But now his job wouldn't be done if raping wasn't included in the daily routine torture. God wouldn't accept his prayers if he doesn't punish the protesters. Freedom isn't something they are allowed to have. He has forgotten what Freedom meant to him. He can't remember his night stands at Ali's, tears of happiness and then their devastating future image.

He has tamed her, she's writing a long fake confession. He wouldn't remember this tomorrow, so what? God is watching. Heaven is waiting.

Ali is in the other room; they call it "The Second Unit" of the city's prison. They say if you get in there, there would be no way back. You'll be gone forever. And that's exactly where he is right now: Nowhere.

He walks in. Ali's tied to the chair. The room is watching, God is watching. Freedom? He's gonna give it to him right away: "You've got two options; die here or go live on television and take back your words." Ali can't tell if he is serious or it is all a big fucking joke. He smiles, just a faint smile and his spinal cord twitches. It takes a couple of seconds to realize the pain. The pain of forbidden love used to be more than this. The memory of the past draws a smile on his face. And it's then that the second one falls on his fingers. He faints.

Darius or better say Ahmed, his new religious name, keeps showing up every seven hours and each time he asks the same questions: Why do you work for western countries? Why do you lead the protests each Tuesday? What do you have on your Facebook page? It is like he can't remember the last time he has been in this room. Ali can't believe the man who was literally torturing him used to be his best friend and his then boyfriend. He has been brain washed. Ali feels helpless; he has to save him himself. So he asks for a pen and paper; he writes anything they want to hear. Confessions that are never true but they are the way out. He crushes his ego, cries of picturing himself as someone he never was. He gets released right away. He flies to the United States as soon as he gets himself together. He is free but his heart is still full of questions and murdered smiles.

Dear Darius,

It's been three months and eleven days that I have not gotten to see you. In the cell, I would wake up every day with bleeding fingers in my pockets, cold and bruised body but a heart full of love and helplessness. I would wish to hear your steps walking in every -I don't know how many- hours and hear you talking to me like you had never known me. It was so sexy. A tough game. The adrenalin rushing through my body, getting deep down to my core would save me. Now here in Boston I don't want to get out of this warm bed knowing I wouldn't hear your voice again. My body alarms every seven hours and makes me lay still and stare at the pillow that used to be yours. I smile at it and wait but there's no hitting after each smile. There's no slapping, no breaking body parts, there's no pain.

I have saved all our photos together in Dena's laptop. I drink my espresso and review each story behind every picture. The last picture of the album is the one I took when you were walking out of the door heading to join the army. I was proud of you, I can memorialize that strong feeling: "My boyfriend was going to save lives" But did you ever save any?

Elaheh Steinke *is a 23-year-old story writer. She studies Genetics at Tehran University and teaches English. Some of her previously published works are* "IWIHKY Disorder", "No Exception", "Falling for the Second Time", "When the Day Is Blue, I'm Sitting Here Wondering about You", "January Went Lost". *She has published her works at Best New Writing 2009 and 2010 and has been the Hoffer award finalist of 2009/2010*

IT'S NOT A MASK

Alexandra Seidel

I collect dead things in my hair
like a child collecting insects' wings
I pull them from the earth
and like a weaver
thread my hair through the hollows of their bones
until they hang
like clinking puppets

My every bow's a rattle
of death
things taken from the twilight
and the stolen clapping of fleshless wrists
laughter's in the sands
and in the rows of seats
fastened to the floor with bolts

my stage is earth
not wood
and time judges my performance, not taste
I wither like a star and drink breath like the moon
My head shakes slowly
as we meet behind the curtain:
one like I does not rehearse

Alexandra Seidel *writes poems and stories of strange things and people, and some of her tales are darker than others. She likes skulls (speaking or otherwise), and loopy has been found a sufficiently descriptive adjective for her. Thanks to some strangely good fortune, her work is (or soon will be) out there:* Bull Spec, Strange Horizons, Scheherezade's Bequest, Goblin Fruit, *and others. Alexandra is the poetry editor for* Niteblade *and the managing editor of* Fantastique Unfettered *and the editor of the* Aether Age eZine. *You can read her blog (which she really tries to update once or twice a month) at www.tigerinthematchstickbox.blogspot.com or follow her on Twitter @Alexa_Seidel.*

Shadows in the Dark

James Turnham

I awoke sweating within the dank, decrepit room that has served as my home for the last four years, its bare walls covered with a foul mould whose odour was quite implacable, an amalgamation of the musty scent of the tomb and expensive perfume. I arose and cast open the heavy, moth-ridden curtains allowing the depressing glow of the dusk to seep in, bloodying the room with reddish haze. Dust swirled and danced as I paced the room watching the door as I always did, listening for the dull reverberating thuds of them. Never had those echoes come but still fear could not be denied. I scarcely left my room in the daylight hours and never when the sun had set below the horizon, silhouetting the bulbous airships which plied their trade between the continents, like I had done, swarming like flies over Haven. I ceased my pacing and studied the ruined city that lay before me. The Great War had not been kind to it, toppled churches shedding noble spires, crumbled manors left with only vestiges of the imperial glory and factory stacks sundered by vengeance.

My gaze returned once more to the airships, following their majestic path as they arced through the sky, wishing for earlier days when I could have been amongst their number. Fate, or perhaps God, felt I was destined for a life of mental frailty and nightmares though my faith had waned since my youth. My God would not allow such abominations as I have looked upon to survive uncontested yet still they lurk within the shadows of my dreams weaving unspeakable horrors.

The bloody glow receded as if defeated and into shadows, the room fell until one could scarcely discern wall from hall. Into dreams I fell, tossing and turning, beckoned by hooded seraphim and cackling daemons until I could endure no more, my soul rent by pity and despair I grasped at the electric light whose cord fell snake-like upon my table. Shadows cast back chased into corners as light bathed the room in sickly aura, half-felt presences vanished and dark whispers became silent, darkness comes and goes but they remain lurking beyond the veil of human senses.

Leaving the light on, I collapsed back into my fitful sleep and found myself once again in that hideous dream-scape from previous nights. I was alone, surrounded by towering structures that rose high leaving me submerged in a world of shadows cut only by slivers of grey light that didn't so much light the world but lessen the shadows that threatened to engulf me. I turned to study the odd hieroglyphics and cartouches that studded the walls as I did every night, like a clockwork automaton, each one making less sense to me than the previous image. I slid my fingers along the stone and recoiled in horror as my finger came away slick with blood, yet the wall gave no outward appearance of this grisly countenance. Disturbed, but with curiosity still left unsatisfied I continued along the narrow alley hoping to come across some doorway or perhaps open plaza, somewhere I could be rid of the terrible claustrophobia that clung to me and pierced my heart with icy tendrils of fear. Ever increasing now, my hands dripped with warm blood, which provided me a hideous trail of breadcrumbs should I come across some turning in this hellish place. My horror was not yet complete, after what felt like hours, I cannot tell for sure for my pocket watch spins mindlessly sometimes carrying time onward at great pace and at others slowing so that the tick of the second became an hour. I came across something that sent a cold tendril to my core, upon the stone flags blood had dripped and dried leaving black stains.

Sunlight struggled through my dirtied windows and forced its way into my closed eyes, dragging me from my tortured slumber the dreams last image remains vivid in my mind's eye black upon grey. You may wonder why my dreams lend me such fear and terror; take heed for within the realm of dreams not all is false and immaterial. I once doubted in the same way many do, but my first trip aboard the Glory ten years ago my eyes were opened. For the first time, did I perceive the first glimpses of the things that lie beyond our own world in dimensions that science has yet to theorize and if the world is merciful shall never probe.

When I signed up with the Glory and her crew of scientists, explorers and treasure hunters, I was still a young man looking to find his fortune within the long ruined cities of the ancient East. Tales told of unfathomable secrets kept within the vaults and sarcophagi of the old kings, but I cared little for such outlandish notions dismissing them as folk-lore, my goal was more material and undoubtedly more selfish. I sought to plunder the dead for coin, let the fools search for books and magic I said, little did I know what kind of fool I was to become and what it would cost me.

The first few months I spent aboard were marred somewhat by the constant cold we were forced to endure as we crossed the mighty spine of mountains that ran between the East and West. When my eyes first clapped upon them, I could scarcely contain my awe. They loomed high into the grey skies cleaving the clouds apart; most peaks were hidden from our gaze. The few that never attained the height of their peers were crowned by a cap of white snow from which jutted mighty spears of obsidian rock, revealing these now calm if imposing precipices of stone to have once filled the skies with smoke and flame like the very furnaces of Hell.

The life of an air-ship lackey is not an easy one nor necessarily long-lived. Dangers are rife in every task; a careless spark could light the Hydrogen tanks above our heads and burn till we are nought but ashes and cinders upon the wind. Or maybe we could be caught in a lightning storm over the self-same, looming mountains that I held in such awe and be dashed against their peaks, created in time immemorial, like pestle on mortar. I was well aware of these dangers and relished in them. As the son of a gentleman, my life had been one of boredom and safety, a terrible fate to one so young; at least that was my view. I took my chance to explore the air-ship that was to become my home for the months to come. My peering did not reassure me of this ships quality, iron bulkheads had long since given over to rust till not much of the original colour--or for that matter strength--remained and the curved balloon showed significant signs of neglect. Great abrasions thinned the silk bag and wore away at the sealant that ensured our flight. I slept uneasily that night, the drones of the twin engines reached a feverish whine as we struggled through the thin mountain air desperately attempting to make head-way against the fierce buffets of wind that tumbled down over the white peaks rocking us this way and that. It screamed through the ill-fitting portholes like the banshee, chilling my bones and flesh but slowly I dropped into a fitful sleep.

By the morning we had cleared the foreboding mountains and had dropped into brilliant sunlight of the surrounding lowlands studded with mesas, spread out beneath us lay crumbling ziggurats, the last vestiges of an empire that stood for a thousand years only to fall to ruin without trace of struggle.

We moored ourselves to one of the more curious structures that rose from the centre of one of the mesa, a pillar of obsidian stone formed into twisting, tentacle-like branches that provided us with a stable anchor point, though we had little idea how it had been erected and its purpose.

Casting our rope ladder down, we descended onto the largest of the mesas upon which stood a weather-stained pyramid. Our captain bade us to climb the great stone steps that lead up to what we assumed to the would be the entrance. As I clambered up the smooth stone, I caught glimpses of cartouches obscured by centuries of moss. My education provided me with knowledge enough to--at least attempt to--discern their meaning but I could glean very little sense from them. I gathered that the pyramid we stood upon had a religious significance as perhaps a place of sacrifice or worship, though in the long dead tongue the two were often interchangeable.

Upon reaching the summit, we marvelled at the vista we beheld. Mountains stretched out across the horizon, crowned with thunder-heads flashing white every few minutes. What lay at our feet held our gaze for still longer, yet for more insidious reasons. The flagons of stone had become stained with the deep red of long dried blood confirming my suspicions as to the nature of this site, yet to my disappointment no obvious entrance could be found. A number of my more emotional shipmates found this site of horrific barbarism somewhat difficult to cope with and gawped in silence. I, however, could see little reason to care about the deaths of long-dead serfs at a time like this: here we stood at the very gates of our dreams and we were more pre-occupied with misplaced sentimentality.

I could bear no more and instead returned to the base of structure searching for some door way or passage that could allow me entrance. After an hour of fruitless exploration, I retired into the shade to shield me from the harsh mid-day sun that beat down relentlessly upon my back, my mind entertaining fancies of what lay within the crumbling monolithic architecture. My thoughts were entirely consumed by riches that I was sure lay buried beneath the ground, encased like the pharaohs. I could bear no more once again; I rose to search for a doorway or crack that had so far eluded me.

The sun had begun to dip below the horizon when I first came upon it, a portal sealed with a slab of solid stone and covered by plant growth. I could scarcely contain my excitement, tearing aside the brush that hid it until I could see the portal in its entirety. I thought perhaps to call upon the aid of my companions but in my greed I held my tongue, why should they gain from my discovery? What lay beneath the pyramid belonged to me and me alone. I set about prising the great stone seal off with the shovel I had brought down along with me. As the stone lifted, I was engulfed by a gust of foetid, stale air causing me to stagger and drop the great stone back into place with an almighty crack. I peered around to see if anyone would bother to check up on my exploits, but to my joy I was alone so once more I braced myself and lifted the stone from its resting place taking care to steel myself against the repeated rushing of air. I managed to knock the stone free from its housing, once again cursing the crash that seemed like the Titans footsteps. I peered down into the cavernous maw-like gap that yawned before me, noting the steps that lead down were carved from the same rock as the bizarre pillar that our airship was now tethered to high above our heads.

I descended feeling the cool, still air brush through my hair. The stairs continued on for some time till I had descended at least ten metres beneath the solid stone. The walls pressed from every side, closing in like a gullet swallowing me whole, until all that remained was inky dark.

I cranked the little electric torch I had thought to bring until it cast out a pathetic flicker of light barely illuminating the room that I now stood in. The whir of the dynamo seemed awfully quiet down here, in this ancient stone sarcophagus. I cast the beam around until it fell upon the far wall from which I recoiled in horror. The wall carvings leered out in grotesque but in eerie life-like ways like the stone had simply grown over them. Tearing my eyes away from the stones I shuddered and hurried down one of the many side corridors that I hoped led to the heart. I cursed myself for not bringing a more sufficient light source, but refused to turn back as by now I would have been missed and perhaps looked for, so I forced my way through the ocean of deep black in my little boat of light.

Time has little meaning under the earth, but after seconds, minutes or even hours and many twists and turns I felt the oppressive ceiling rise away and allow a little light through some unseen crack allowing me to look upon the labyrinthine corridors in proper. The walls were hewn from rough stone like much else I had seen but had little of the exquisite craftsmanship that I assumed was the norm. Placing my torch in my coat pocket, I began studying the cartouches and glyphs similar to the ones I had seen before but changed somehow, the life-like qualities had given way to a disturbing wrongness; they seemed to writhe and shift under one's gaze like a serpent. I quickly attributed such thoughts to folly and tiredness and decided that I needed to rest, at least for a few minutes. I sat and propped myself against the wall where upon a sudden drowsiness came over me like a wave breaking upon the beach.

I jerked awake and quickly gathered myself but something seemed amiss, the grey light I had been using had dimmed. I fumbled in my pockets for the torch but found nothing. I forced myself to remain calm and thoroughly searched the ground around me in case it had spilled from my pockets while I dozed but still found nothing. Perhaps my crew had indeed come looking for me, discovered the doorway, followed the winding corridors just as I had and upon discovering my slumbering body decided that my selfishness should be repaid. I called out politely at first but the façade soon crumbled as I unleashed a torrent of curses on both them and their misbegotten hides. To all my shouting the only reply I received was from myself as the echoes bounced around me, fury slowly gave way to fear. I fumed at my own stupidity, why had I not brought a second torch? Some matches? Anything was better than the rapidly declining ambient light. I studied the glyphs, hoping for some clue that would allow me to find my way out but none was forth-coming. My hand brushed against the wall but the rough surface was replaced by wet and slickness, I glanced down and my blood chilled. Through the wall, blood seeped until the stone was painted red. I stood, mouth wide in sheer, unbridled terror, my rational mind had shut down leaving only primal instincts. I ran, blood-dripping from my hands, sprinting head-long through the dark scarcely caring where I went just so long as it was away from there.

Slowly my mind returned and the animal retreated back into the depths of my mind but what I came across next almost shattered what little sanity I had left. In front of me, drops of blood had dried upon floor. My mind raced, how had I been running in circles? Had I managed to miss off-shooting passages? I swayed on the spot, exhaustion sapped my strength and it was all I could do to not collapse. But that was the least of my worries; the light had finally gone, leaving the dark to engulf me.

I don't know how long I just stood there, reeling, but I was wrenched from my thoughts by a quiet noise almost on the edge of hearing like the sound of a thousand breaths and then slow dripping slowly getting faster and faster. I reached out in front of me only to be confounded by solid rock, to my horror this happened on every side, I was trapped, locked in a nightmare tomb. Liquid surrounded my feet and I could feel it rising, slowly but inexorably. I trashed and beat upon the walls of my tomb until my blood and tears mixed with whatever was coming up through the floor and screamed long after my hands had been become useless. The water reached my nose and forced its way down my throat, suffocating me until my lungs gave out and mercifully allowed me to descend into blissful unconsciousness.

My eyes opened and I felt dry as bone but coughing water. I screamed at the hidden malevolence, begging it to come forward and end the torment. To this day, the response haunts me, from the shadows slunk hideously scaled and malformed beasts--some were bi-pedal--others slithered obscenely across the smooth stone floor on which I had found myself. From their mouths issued forth maniacal gibbering, raucous laughter mocking me, taunting me. I was bound to the spot where I lay compelled by unseen chains to stay, whispering obscenities closer they drew until their foetid breath blew across my neck and crusted talons scraped along my flesh.

"We are sin." They said "We are your beginning, your end, the alpha and omega, first and last and now you are ours and we do so like to play with our food".

James Turnham *is an aspiring author from a village in rural England and spends his time juggling his studies and writing short stories that for some bizarre reason people enjoy reading. He hopes to one day make a career out of his writing whether it be as an 'artiste' writing fiction outside of Parisian cafés, slowly drowning himself in cheap coffee or working as a freelance journalist writing about terribly important things that have happened in theworld that in all honesty he has no idea about.*

Subscribe to

BÊTE NOIRE

1 year, 4 issues
$23.95*

Send email to: subscribe @betenoiremagazine.com
Or fill out the form below and send, along with check or
money order made payable to Jennifer Gifford to:

P.O. Box 1013
Grayson, GA 30017

Name:_____

Address: _____

Email:_____

Susbcription includes Dark Opus Press's annual anthnology

*US and Canada only, international subscriptions $29.95/year

11513493R00034

Made in the USA
Charleston, SC
01 March 2012